This book is dedicated to **Evva Friason,** a woman who loves fiercely, and to her grandchildren, **Kristin & Lawrence**, who love unconditionally.

2020: Year 10 of Living with Dementia

www.mascotbooks.com

Does Grandma Remember Me?

©2021 Evita Sherman. All Rights Reserved. No part of this publication may be reproduced, stored in a retrieval system or transmitted in any form by any means electronic, mechanical, or photocopying, recording or otherwise without the permission of the author.

To obtain permission, contact Evita Sherman through the "Contact" tab on her website: evitasherman.com

For more information, please contact:
Mascot Books
620 Herndon Parkway, Suite 320
Herndon, VA 20170
info@mascotbooks.com

Library of Congress Control Number: 2020908079

CPSIA Code: PRT1020A
ISBN-13: 978-1-64543-529-7

Printed in the United States

My Grandma is very special.
She is the best cook! Everything she makes is delicious, and she doesn't even use a recipe.

One thing I love to do is sit on Grandma's lap and look into her big, brown eyes. She always makes me smile.

Then, she grabs me in a big bear hug and kisses my forehead, singing, ♪ **"You're the best granddaughter in the world."** ♪

When she smiles back at me, Grandma makes me feel like I'm the only little girl on Earth. Grandma is proud of me for everything, even when I do something small.

But now she is not the same.
She's different.

Sometimes, she looks at me like she doesn't know me.
But how could Grandma not know me?
I'm her little **ANGEL!**

She frowns when she used to smile.
I can't sit on her lap for very long
because...

She jumps up from the breakfast table
and looks through every kitchen cabinet
like she's lost something.

But she never finds it.

I wish there was a recipe that could help my Grandma now.

She dumps everything out of her purse ten times,
and I help her put it all back...

Then, she asks, "What am I looking for?"

Grandma knows I can't tell time yet. But she still asks me at least fifty times, "What time is it?"

Mommy tells us the time, but then Grandma looks worried like she doesn't understand.
Mommy says Grandma has a disease called dementia. Dementia attacks people's brains and stops them from remembering parts of their life.

It's not that they don't want to remember or that they don't love you in the same way they once did.

Their brains just won't let them.

For days I was a very sad little girl.

But one day, I thought how lucky I am that dementia doesn't make ME forget **how to show my Grandma that I love her.**

I'll keep holding her hand.
I'll keep hugging her tightly.
I'll keep kissing her cheek the way
she used to kiss mine.

One day, Grandma may not remember me, but she'll always know I love her by **the way *I* make *her* feel.**

Grandma can be different.

But I'll be the same.

The same little angel who loves her Grandma.

Evita Sherman and her mother

About the Author

Evita's passion is assisting the elderly, especially those living with dementia. Her mission is to help people age in the manner they envision for themselves and not through the lens of others. She works to provide data and resources to assist elders in effectively aging-in-place and equips their families and friends to support their loved ones amidst uncertainty.

Working in the elder care field as a licensed nursing home administrator, senior living marketing professional, and Certified Aging-in-Place Specialist (CAPS), Evita witnesses both elders and families make tough decisions. Some of those decisions result in despair, while others result in healing. The key to enabling elders to live life to its fullest is to help them find their voices and exercise their right to choose.

Evita collaborates with family and friends to ensure that her mother, who lives with dementia, and her father, recently diagnosed with mild cognitive impairment, maintain their voices and make well-informed choices as their disease progresses.

Acknowledgments

I wish to thank those who endured all my drafts and contributed to making this book come to life.

Your daily inspiration, ideas, and support make me feel like I can be Superwoman.

Thank you, Ilene K. Lockman, for having a PhD in "Ideas" and always sharing them. Paul Pierce, I appreciate you for your online hook-up, great editing style, and boatloads of love and kindness, always.

Taking a leap of faith to write this book allowed me to stumble upon a very creative, young illustrator within my extended family. Chayla, I am indebted to you for making this book come alive. My mother would approve!